CALL
SUPER HERO HIGH SCHOOL
S H H S
SUPER HERO HIGH SCHOOL
KATANA
SUPER-POWERS
Champion Samurai sword fighter, expert martial artist, painter
SUPER HERO HIGH SCHOOL
BEAST BOY
SUPER-POWERS
Shape shifts into any animal form, world-class slacker
SUPER HERO HIGH
AMANDA WALLER
Principal
STAFF
SUPER HERO HIGH SCHOOL
GORILLA GRODD
Vice-principal
STAFF

DC SUPER HERO GIRLS™

FINALS CRISIS

an original graphic novel

WRITTEN BY **Shea Fontana**

ART BY **Yancey Labat**

COLORS BY **Monica Kubina**

LETTERING BY **Janice Chiang**

DC SUPER HERO GIRLS: FINALS CRISIS. July, 2016.
Published by DC Comics, 2900 W. Alameda Avenue, Burbank, CA 91505. GST # is R125921072.

This book is manufactured at a facility holding chain-of-custody certification. This paper is made with sustainably managed North American fiber. For Advertising and Custom Publishing contact dccomicsadvertising@dccomics.com. For details on DC Comics Ratings, visit dccomics.com/go/ratings.
Printed by Transcontinental Interglobe, Beauceville, QC, Canada. 12/14/17. Third Printing.
ISBN: 978-1-4012-6247-1

TABLE OF CONTENTS

ROLL

SUPER HERO HIGH SCHOOL
S H H S
WONDER WOMAN
SUPER-POWERS
Super-strength, flight, near-invincibility, super-athleticism
SUPER HERO HIGH SCHOOL
S H H S
SUPERGIRL
SUPER-POWERS
Super-strength, flight, invincibility, super-hearing, heat vision, x-ray vision
SUPER HERO HIGH SC
S H H S
BATGIRL
SUPER-POWERS
Computer genius, expert martial artist, photographic memory, legendary detective skills
SUPER HERO HIGH SCHOOL
S H H S
BUMBLEBEE
SUPER-POWERS
Enhanced strength, flight, ability to shrink, projects stinger blasts
SUPER HERO HIGH SC
S H H S
POISON IVY
SUPER-POWERS
Genius-level intellect, summons and controls plants

chapter one
SUPER HERO HIGH

CHEETAH AND I USED TO BE FRIENDS.
WELL, NOT *FRIENDS* FRIENDS.
SNARRRRRRL!
BUT, IF I SAW HER AT CAPES & COWLS CAFÉ AFTER SCHOOL, I'D PROBABLY WAVE.
SCRATCHH
BUT NOW, I MUST TREAT HER AS *MY ENEMY.*

RAAAWWWR!
SHE'S FAST.

BUT I'M A LITTLE FASTER.
HEY! NOT FAIR!
SORRY, CHEETAH. AS THEY SAY, ALL IS FAIR IN...
...LOVE...
...WAR...

...AND COACH WILDCAT'S P.E. CLASS.
RRRRIIIIING!
THAT'S THE BELL! NICE SPARRING, WONDER WOMAN!
WONDER WOMAN
A
WOO!
AWESOME!
HISSSSSS!
LOVED THE MOVES!
THANKS, COACH!
SEE YOU AT FINALS TOMORROW!

ALL STUDENTS REPORT TO THE AUDITORIUM.
LATER...
SHUT YER TEETH TRAPS AND OPEN YER EAR HOLES!
PRINCIPAL WALLER'S GOT AN ANNOUNCEMENT.
THANK YOU, VICE PRINCIPAL GRODD.
STUDENTS, AS YOU KNOW, TOMORROW IS SEMESTER FINALS.

TO PASS, YOU MUST DEMONSTRATE THAT YOUR POWERS HAVE IMPROVED SINCE YOUR ENTRANCE EVALUATION.
FINALS BEGIN TOMORROW AT NINE. DO NOT BE LATE.
ORACLE, SET ALARM FOR TOMORROW AT NINE.
AS YOU WISH.
9:00
FINALS
NOW GET YER BUTTS BACK INTO CLASS!
OUR LAST INTRO TO SUPER-SUITS CLASS BEFORE FINALS!
READY TO GET YOUR "EVENING WEAR" ON?
UH-OH!
I, UM, LEFT MY STEALTH-SUIT PROJECT IN MY LOCKER!
GOTTA GO!

RRRRRIIIIIING!
EMERGENCY!
EMERGENCY!
WHAT'S WRONG, MR. CRAZY QUILT?
EMERGENCY OF THE WORST SORT!

A FASHION EMERGENCY!
WELL, I THINK YOU'RE JUST BEING A TRENDSETTER!
THANK YOU, WONDER WOMAN! I AM A TRENDSETTER, AREN'T I? NOW TIME TO TAKE ROLL! KATANA?
HERE!
HARLEY QUINN?
RIGHT HERE, CRAZE!
THAT'S MISTER QUILT TO YOU!
SURE THING, MISTAH Q!
SUPERGIRL?
ANYONE SEEN SUPERGIRL?
NOPE.
NOT ME.
LAST I SAW HER WAS IN WEAPONOMICS.

UM...
...I THINK SHE WASN'T FEELING WELL...
"...YEAH, THAT'S IT!"
TO BE CONTINUED.

chapter two

HOMEWORK

I HAD TO GET OUT OF THERE.
SMALLVILLE.
WHEN I SEE THE KENT FARM, THE KNOTS IN MY STOMACH FINALLY START TO UNWIND.
NONE OF THAT SUPER HERO HIGH STUFF CAN BOTHER ME HERE.
SUPERGIRL?
AAAGH!!

CRASSH
MOOOOOO!
SORRY, BELLE!
GEE WILLIKERS! I THOUGHT ANOTHER SPACESHIP CRASHED INTO THE BARN!
KARA! ARE YOU OKAY?
YEAH--UNCLE JONATHAN JUST CAME OUT OF NOWHERE AND SCARED ME, THEN...OOPS!
WHAT HAPPENED?
AUNT MARTHA, I HAVE BIG NEWS. I'M QUITTING SCHOOL.
BUT WHY ARE YOU HERE? SHOULDN'T YOU BE AT SCHOOL?
NOTHING YET.
BUT SOMETHING'S COMING.
SOMETHING BAD.

IT'S FINALS!
TESTS WERE MY KRYPTONITE EVEN BEFORE KRYPTONITE WAS MY KRYPTONITE!
SUPERGIRL, YOU'VE FOUGHT VILLAINS AND SAVED SUPER HERO HIGH MORE TIMES THAN I CAN COUNT!
THAT'S RIGHT! A LITTLE TEST CAN'T BE THAT BAD.
OH, YEAH?

KRYPTON, THEN...
GOOD LUCK ON YOUR PRESENTATION, KARA!*
THANKS, MOM!
IT ALL STARTED BACK HOME ON KRYPTON.
*TRANSLATED FROM KRYPTONIAN.
THIS WAS BEFORE THE KRYPTONIAN COUNSEL REALIZED THE PLANET WAS DOOMED...
BEFORE MY PARENTS BUILT THE SPACESHIP THAT WOULD BRING ME TO SAFETY, HERE ON EARTH...
...AND BEFORE I GOT SUCKED THROUGH A WORMHOLE THAT MADE ME FALL A FEW DECADES BEHIND ON MY ESTIMATED EARTH ARRIVAL TIME.
C'MON, COMET!
IT SEEMED LIKE FINALS DAY AT KRYPTON HIGH WOULD BE JUST ANOTHER NORMAL DAY FOR NORMAL ME.

AT LEAST, I FELT LIKE NORMAL ME. I DIDN'T HAVE ANY SUPERPOWERS-- NO ONE DID ON KRYPTON!
BUT EVEN WITHOUT POWERS, I GUESS I WAS DIFFERENT FROM OTHER KIDS.
OH MY RAO! LOOK AT KARA!
WHO WANTS A HORSE WHEN YOU CAN HOVER?
LAAAAME!
HEY, KARA, EORX 8999 TELECOMMUNICATED. THEY WANT THEIR MODE OF TRANSPORTATION BACK!
HAHAHAHAHA!

LOOK, KARA'S MOMMY PUT HER HOUSE NAME ON HER BAG! WOULDN'T WANT LITTLE KARA TO LOSE IT!
HA HA HA HA HA!
WHAT A WEAKLING!
WHOA!
MAMA'S GIRL!
RRRRRRING!
SPLASH
YOU'LL BE UP FIRST, KARA.
SORRY I'M LATE!

-GULP-
FOR MY SCIENCE CLASS FINAL, I'VE COME UP WITH A NEW, FASTER WAY OF GROWING CRYSTALS!
JUST ADD A TINY DROP OF MY SOLUTION TO THE CRYSTAL...
AND THE CRYSTAL TRIPLES IN SIZE!
I HAD PRACTICED MY PRESENTATION OVER AND OVER AGAIN.
COOL!
WHOA!
SHE DID IT!
IT WAS GOING REALLY WELL.
SHE REALLY DID IT!
HA HA HA HA!
UNTIL...

OH NO!
COMET!
SMAASH
COMET, COME BACK!
HAHAHA!
I WANTED MY PRESENTATION TO KNOCK THEM OUT OF THEIR SEATS...
HSSSSSSSSS

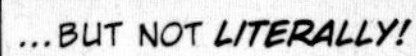
...BUT NOT *LITERALLY!*
KKKRRRAAKKKKK!

YOU'RE GOING TO BE OKAY.
BUT I'M NOT.
UM, AT LEAST MY SOLUTION WORKED. DOES THAT MEAN I PASSED?
I HAVE NEVER SEEN SUCH CARELESSNESS AND NEGLECT! YOU'RE LUCKY NO ONE GOT HURT!
KARA ZOR-EL
*◊ IS KRYPTONIAN FOR "F"
BUT...BUT... BUT...

SMALLVILLE, NOW...
YOU POOR THING!
IF THOSE GIRLS WERE HERE RIGHT NOW, I'D GIVE THEM A PIECE OF MY MIND!
THAT'S WHY I CAN'T GO BACK TO SUPER HERO HIGH. WHAT IF IT HAPPENS AGAIN!?
AW, PUMPKIN! IF YOU DON'T GO BACK AND GIVE THOSE FINALS EVERYTHING YOU GOT, THEN THOSE BULLIES WIN!
YOU'RE RIGHT. I HAVE TO TAKE THAT TEST! NOBODY CAN STOP ME!
GOOD LUCK ON YOUR FINALS, DEAR!
I DON'T NEED LUCK. I'M GONNA KICK SOME FINALS BUTT!
HEY, LANGUAGE, SUPERGIRL!

TARGET
SPOTTED.
IF YOU KNOW WHERE TO LOOK, YOU CAN GET ANYTHING ON THE INTERNET.
VOOOOSHHH!
EVEN KRYPTONITE.

OOOOOOOO
ONE DOWN. FIVE TO GO.
SUPERGIRL
WONDER WOMAN
BUMBLEBEE
KATANA
BATGIRL
IVY
TO BE CONTINUED.

chapter three

GROWING UP

MEANWHILE...
AND MY STEALTH-WEAR WOULDN'T BE COMPLETE WITHOUT AN ENHANCED UTILITY BELT.
THIS ASSIGNMENT IS ALL ABOUT TECH, BUT I DON'T DO THAT.
INSTEAD OF WIRES, MICROCHIPS AND STEEL, I USE LEAVES, VINES AND CHLOROPHYLL.
EXCELLENT WORK, BATGIRL!
RRRRIIIIING!
GOOD LUCK AT FINALS TOMORROW, MY LITTLE SUPERLETS!

TOPSY-TURVY THAT FROWN, IVY!
CAN'T. I HAVE--
AGAIN?
DETENTIO
WHAT'D YA DO THIS TIME?
IT WASN'T THAT BAD...

YESTERDAY...
I DO NOT HAVE THE EIGHT. YOU, GO TO THE FISH!
CRRACKOOM!
RAAAAA!

RAAAAAAAA!
I DO NOT APPRECIATE THE ATTACK OF THE SHRUBBERY!
THIS IS WHAT I GET FOR BEING A VEGETARIAN!

NICE WORK, CHOMPY!
NOW...
ALL I DID WAS USE A TEENY BIT TOO MUCH FERTILIZER.
NO GRINNING IN DETENTION!
YOU NEED TO KEEP YER VEG UNDER CONTROL, OR YOU'LL BE SPENDIN' EVERY AFTERNOON IN DETENTION!
-:-SIGH.-:-

I CAN'T WAIT 'TIL I GRADUATE. THEN, I CAN DO WHATEVER I WANT AND NEVER HAVE TO WILT AWAY IN DETENTION.
WHY WAIT?
TOMORROW'S FINALS ARE ALL ABOUT SHOWING THAT YOUR POWERS HAVE IMPROVED, RIGHT?
YEAH, BUT I'M NOT WORRIED ABOUT FINALS. IN THE TIME I'VE BEEN AT SUPER HERO HIGH, MY POWERS HAVE REALLY GROWN.
PROVE IT. GO ALL OUT. CRANK UP THE FERTILIZER!
YEAH! FOR MY FINALS DEMO, I'LL HAVE THE BIGGEST, WILDEST PLANT EVER!
HEY!
I SAID NO GRINNIN'!

LATER...
EVER SINCE I LAID EYES ON YOU, I KNEW YOU WERE MORE THAN JUST A HOUSEPLANT!
THAT'S WHY I WENT OUT ON A LIMB TO LIBERATE YOU FROM PRINCIPAL WALLER'S OFFICE!
ONCE I GET YOU IN MY GREENHOUSE AND ADD MY IVY TOUCH, YOU'LL BE MY MOST MASSIVE PLANT EVER!

MEGA SALE!!! 50% OFF ALL RADIOACTIVELY ENHANCED SUPER-GROW FERTILIZER!
MEGA SALE!!! 50% OFF ALL RADIOACTIVELY ENHANCED SUPER-GROW FERTILIZER!
MISTER GREENBERG, IT'S YOUR *LUCKY* DAY!

CAPES & COWLS
CAFE
METROPOLIS
BANK
JAVINS AVE
HOLZHERR
METROPOLIS
BANK
JAVINS AVE
HOLZHERR

ORP
GARDEN SUPPLY
GUESS IT MAKES SENSE TO BUY FERTILIZER IN SUCH A SEEDY PLACE.
MEGA SALE!!! 50% OFF ALL RADIOACTIVELY ENHANCED SUPER-GROW FERTILIZER!
CLICK!
HELLO, IVY.

I'VE BEEN TRAINING FOR THIS ALL SEMESTER.
YAH!
DRILL AFTER DRILL AFTER BORING DRILL TO PERFECT MY SUPERPOWERS.
BUT THAT WAS AT SCHOOL, WITH ITS MANICURED LAWNS, DEPENDABLE HEDGES AND A SAD SUCCULENT SUFFERING ON EVERY TEACHER'S DESK.
WE EVEN HAVE AN ORGANIC KITCHEN GARDEN FOR THE CAFETERIA!
BUT THIS PLACE HAS BEEN SANITIZED. NOTHING'S GROWING HERE. NOT EVEN FUNGUS-- UNLESS YOU COUNT THE CREEPER WHO LURED ME HERE.
CLANK!
CLANK!
CLANK!
CLANK!

ERGH!
K-CHINNNG!
VRRRRSSSSS
KLANG!
SSSH!

LET ME PUT THIS IN TERMS YOU CAN ***UNDERSTAND.***
YOU'VE BEEN A ***THORN*** IN MY SIDE, AND I'M ***PRUNING*** YOU FROM SUPER HERO HIGH.
TO BE CONTINUED.

chapter four
ON THE SNACK RUN

I GOT MY SUPER-SUIT TUNED UP.
AND MY BATTERY CHARGED.
NOW, ALL I NEED IS ONE MORE NIGHT OF CRAMMING BEFORE FINALS.
STARFIRE, WHO WROTE "THE HISTORY OF HEROES"?
LIBERTY BELLE! THAT QUESTION WAS THE EASY OF PEAS!

BUMBLEBEE, NAME THE THREE POWS.
SUPERPOWER, BRAINPOWER AND... UM...ER...
GRRRRRRRRRRRRR!
WHAT WAS THAT?
COULD IT BE THE MAN OF THE BOOGEY!?
WELL, ALL I NEED IS ONE MORE NIGHT OF CRAMMING AND A HONEY SMOOTHIE!
IT'S JUST MY TUMMY!
THERE IS A BOOGEY IN YOUR STOMACH?
NO, I'M HUNGRY! CAN'T STUDY FOR FINALS ON AN EMPTY STOMACH.
BUT WE HAVE 765 MORE FLASHCARDS TO GET THROUGH!
DON'T WORRY, FLASH. I'M GONNA GRAB SOME GRUB FROM CAPES & COWLS CAFÉ, AND I'LL B.R.B.

SNNNNARRRL!
HELP! THIEF!

NOBODY GETS BETWEEN ME AND MY SMOOTHIE!
BUMBLEBEE STING!
ZZZZOOOSSSSSSH!
SNARL!
EEK!
TINY TIME!
CAN'T CATCH ME, CROC!
HUH?

MESS WITH THE BEE--
--AND YOU'RE GONNA GET STUNG!
OOGGG!

WOW!
WAY TO HERO, BUMBLEBEE!
YEAH, HONEY!
HOW DOES IT FEEL TO HAVE SINGLE-HANDEDLY STOPPED CROC FROM STEALING THOSE TUNA FISH SANDWICHES?
WELL, LOIS, I FEEL A LOT LIKE I FELT WHEN I CAME IN HERE-- HUNGRY!
HOW 'BOUT WHIPPING ME UP ONE OF YOUR HONEY SMOOTHIES WHILE WE WAIT FOR METROPOLIS S.C.U.* TO PICK UP THE OVERGROWN LIZARD?
SORRY, NO CAN DO.
*SPECIAL CRIMES UNIT
STEVE
STEVE

GUESS YOUR ELECTRIC STINGS ARE AS GOOD AT TAKING OUT SMOOTHIE MACHINES AS THEY ARE AT TAKING OUT VILLAINS.
STEVE
I BUILT MY SUPER-SUIT--FIXING A SMOOTHIE MACHINE SHOULD BE **NO PROBLEM!**

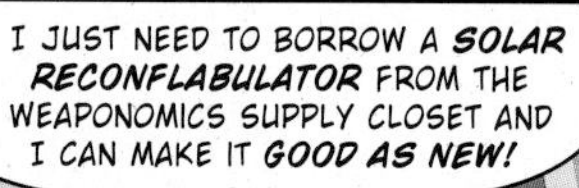
I JUST NEED TO BORROW A ***SOLAR RECONFLABULATOR*** FROM THE WEAPONOMICS SUPPLY CLOSET AND I CAN MAKE IT ***GOOD AS NEW!***

MISTER FOX?

NO FOX HERE. JUST **ME,** GETTIN' MY GOAT ON.
EEK! BEAST BOY! WHY WERE YOU HIDING?
SHHH! KATANA'S COMING!
ARE YOU AND KATANA PLAYING **SUPER HIDE-AND-SEEK** AGAIN?
YOU **KNOW** IT, DOUBLE-B!

I WON'T TELL KATANA YOU'RE HERE. I JUST NEED TO GRAB THE SOLAR RECONFLABULATOR AND I'LL BE OUT OF YOUR HAIR--ER, FUR.
YOU SURE YOU HAVEN'T SEEN MISTER FOX? I NEED HIS SIGNATURE SO I CAN BORROW THIS.
Tool sign out sheet
Mandatory - Mr. Fox
Name
Tool
Signature
NO TRACE OF THE DUDE SINCE I'VE BEEN HERE.
IT IS LATE. HE PROBABLY BUZZED OFF HOURS AGO.
GUESS YOU'LL HAVE TO WAIT 'TIL TOMORROW, YO.
I'LL JUST FIX THE SMOOTHIE MACHINE AND BRING THIS BACK BEFORE ANYONE KNOWS IT'S GONE!
MISTER FOX DOESN'T REALLY NEED TO APPROVE THAT, RIGHT?
GRROWWL!

SHOOOSSH!
KRINK!
MY WORK IS DONE HERE.
WAYNE TECHNOLOGIES
ZZZRRR!
IT'S ON THE HOUSE!
SWEET! THANKS, STEVE!

CREAMY!

SWEET!

DELICIOUS!

OH, YEAAAAAH.

WHAT'S THAT!?!

SMELLS LIKE HONEY COOKIES! AND HONEY CAKE!

AND HONEY LATTES!

I'D SAY THAT WAS AS EASY AS LURING A BEE TO HONEY, BUT THAT SEEMS AWFULLY ON THE NOSE.
URGH!

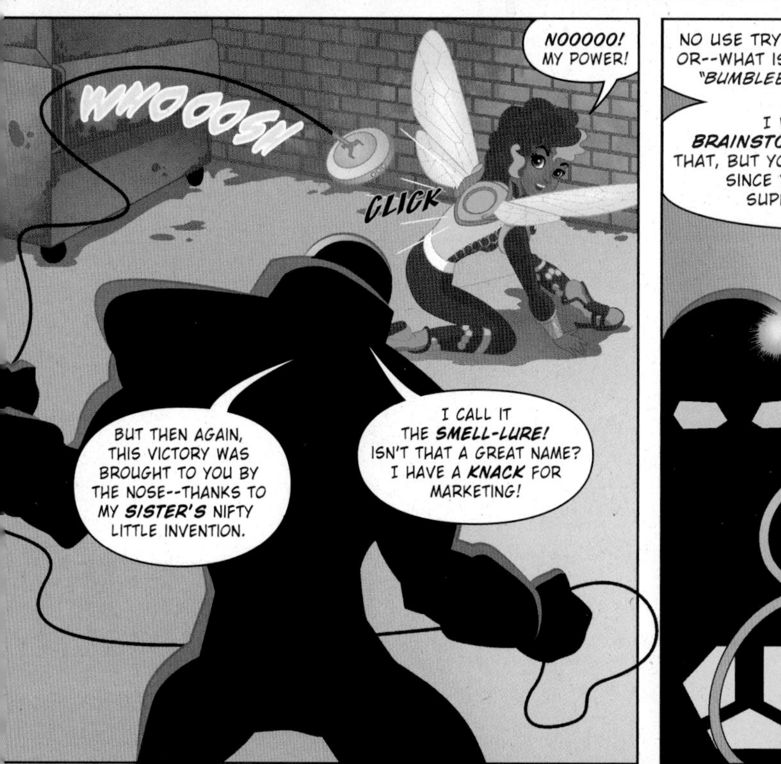
WHOOOSH
NOOOOO! MY POWER!
CLICK
BUT THEN AGAIN, THIS VICTORY WAS BROUGHT TO YOU BY THE NOSE--THANKS TO MY SISTER'S NIFTY LITTLE INVENTION.
I CALL IT THE SMELL-LURE! ISN'T THAT A GREAT NAME? I HAVE A KNACK FOR MARKETING!

NO USE TRYING TO SHRINK OR FLY OR--WHAT IS IT YOU CALL THAT?--"BUMBLEBEE STING"? ICK!
I WOULD HELP YOU BRAINSTORM A BETTER NAME FOR THAT, BUT YOU WON'T NEED IT ANYMORE SINCE YOU'LL NEVER HAVE SUPERPOWERS AGAIN!

-HHHHPHH!-
ANOTHER PEST FOR MY COLLECTION.
TO BEE CONTINUED.

chapter five

SLICE OF LIFE

THIS PAST SEMESTER AT SUPER HERO HIGH, I'VE HONED MY POWERS LIKE I HONE MY SWORD...
...NON-STOP!
EACH SWING OF MY SWORD MAKES MY MIND AND BODY SHARPER, MORE PREPARED TO CUT THROUGH TOMORROW'S FINALS.

LAY IT ON ME!
HAIII--
BEAST BOY IS THE PERFECT PRACTICE PARTNER. HE'S QUICK, FUN AND TOTES UNPREDICTABLE.
WOOOSH!
--YAH!
ANY WAY YOU SLICE IT, BEAST BOY IS A CUT ABOVE.

TOO LOW, SLOWPOKE!
BRING IT ON, LITTLE CRITTER!

GOTCHA!
GAME OVER, MAN!

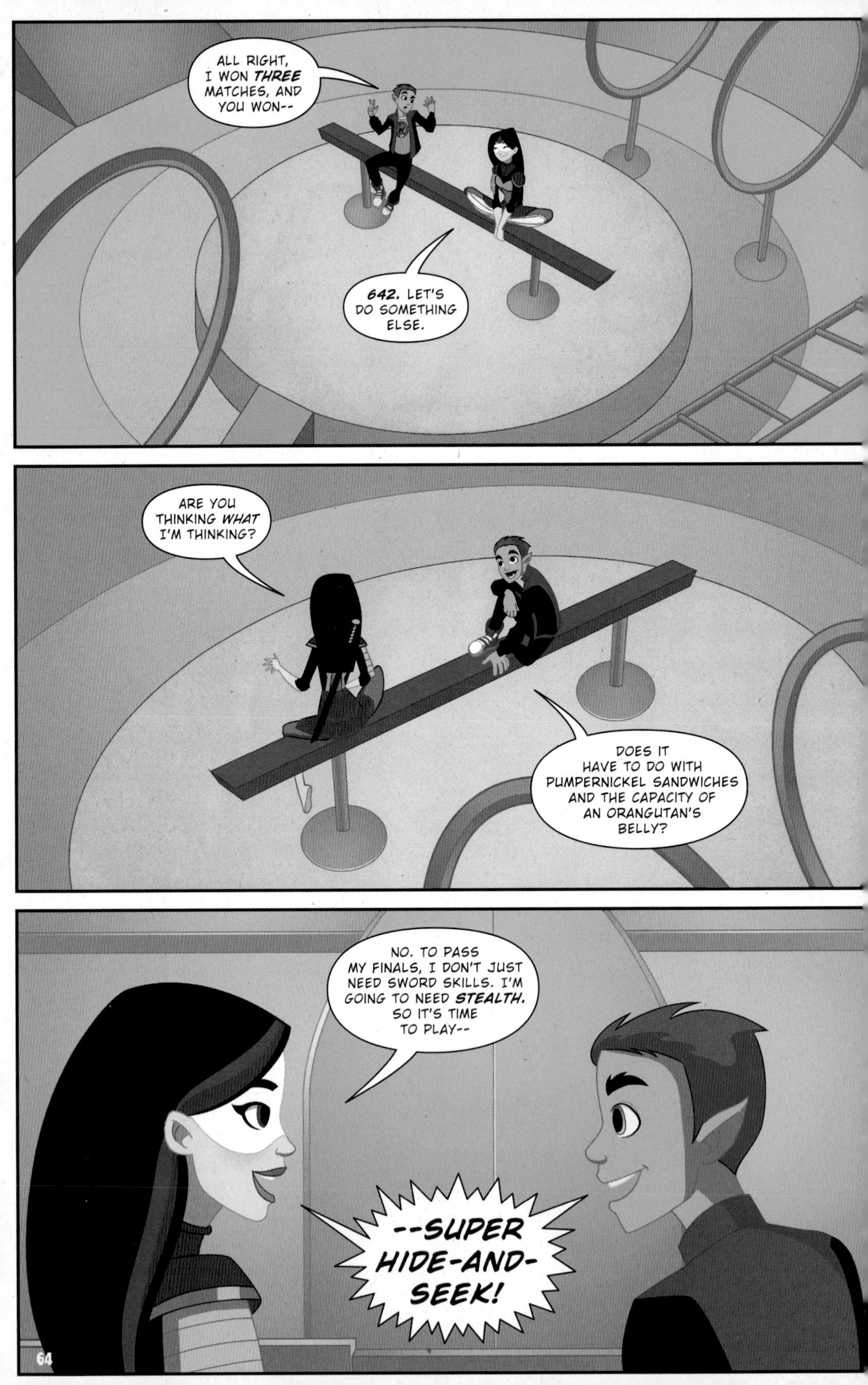
ALL RIGHT, I WON THREE MATCHES, AND YOU WON--
642. LET'S DO SOMETHING ELSE.
ARE YOU THINKING WHAT I'M THINKING?
DOES IT HAVE TO DO WITH PUMPERNICKEL SANDWICHES AND THE CAPACITY OF AN ORANGUTAN'S BELLY?
NO. TO PASS MY FINALS, I DON'T JUST NEED SWORD SKILLS. I'M GOING TO NEED STEALTH. SO IT'S TIME TO PLAY--
--SUPER HIDE-AND-SEEK!

FOUND YOU!
AW, MAN!
TOO EASY!
ZINNG!
GOTCHA AGAIN!

NO WAY--
AMANDA WALLER

--KATANA WILL FIND ME *HERE!*
AMANDA WALLER
STRIKE SQUAD, BOWL REVE TOURNAMENT

HI!
AAAAGH!

AHH! POINTY!
SLICE
PRINCIPAL WALLER'S GONNA GIVE US A DETENTION LIFE SENTENCE! WHAT ARE WE GONNA DO?
WE HAVE TO FIX IT!

HOT GLUE.
LOOKS GOOD TO THESE HAWK EYES!
LET'S GET IT BACK TO THE PRINCIPAL'S OFFICE.
WE'VE GOT WALLER TO THE LEFT.
BEAST BOY, YOU DISTRACT PRINCIPAL WALLER. I'LL REPLACE THE TROPHY.
YOU GOT IT, BOSS LADY!

WOOOO-HOOOOO!
NO SKATEBOARDING IN THE HALL!
CROC AT THE CAPES & COWLS CAFÉ? I'LL BE RIGHT THERE!

WHEW!
HUFF.
GOOD AS NEW!
HUH? WHO--?

SHNK!
DON'T YOU LIKE MY SUIT'S STEALTH TECHNOLOGY? YOU DIDN'T EVEN HEAR ME!
UHN!
MY SUIT ALSO HAS HIGH SPEED, REACTIVE MOVEMENT! ISN'T THAT COOL?

Lex Corp
HEY, KATANA, IS COUNTRY OKAY? OR WOULD YOU *PREFER* SOMETHING RELAXING, LIKE SMOOTH JAZZ?

LET ME OUT OF HERE RIGHT NOW!
SMOOTH JAZZ IT IS!
WONDER WOMAN
BUMBLEBEE
KATANA
BATGIRL
IVY
TO BE CONTINUED.

chapter six
EXTRA CREDIT

METROPOLIS IS SO DIFFERENT FROM THEMYSCIRA, THE ISLAND WHERE I GREW UP.
STAR LABS
THE CITY'S FULL OF CONTRADICTIONS. THE DARKNESS OF THE NIGHT ALLOWS US TO SEE THE BEAUTY OF THE CITY LIGHTS--
--BUT IT ALSO HIDES THE DANGER THAT LURKS AT NIGHT.
WELL, DANGER *USUALLY* LURKS AT NIGHT. TONIGHT'S BEEN SLOW.
HOW DID YOU DO ON MISTER FOX'S WEAPONOMICS POP QUIZ?
100 PERCENT.
I ELEVATED THE COMMON CORE QUIZ TO EXTRAORDINAR HEIGHTS WITH MY PERFECT ANSWERS!
GUESS THAT MEANS WE'RE STILL TIED FOR TOP OF THE CLASS.
AT LEAST UNTIL FINALS TOMORROW.

WHY DON'T YOU TWO GO IN AND STUDY? I CAN KEEP LOOKOUT HERE.
AND LET YOU GET ALL THE EXTRA CREDIT? NO WAY, HAWKGIRL!
LADY SHIVA TOLERATES NO ONE SURPASSING HER IN EXTRA CREDIT!
EIGHT O'CLOCK.
ONLY THIRTEEN HOURS UNTIL FINALS.
WHICH IS PLENTY OF TIME TO GET IN SOME EXTRA CREDIT VILLAIN BUTT KICKING!
BUT WHERE WILL WE FIND A VILLAIN WORTHY OF OUR EXTRA CREDIT EFFORTS?
GIGANTA!
YES, WONDER WOMAN, GIGANTA WOULD BE A FINE OPPONENT, BUT WE CANNOT FORCE HER TO SHOW HERSELF--
HELLO, EXTRA CREDIT!
--OH, YOU MEANT GIGANTA'S IN METROPOLIS!

LET'S GO, SUPER HERO GIRLS!

I SAID, "NO WHIPPED CREAM!"
T-T-THIS ONE'S YOURS! YOU TOOK THE WRONG ONE!
RRRRR.
LOIS
NO LITTLE MAN TELLS GIGANTA SHE DID WRONG!
HELP! SOMEBODY HELP ME!

HUH?!
PUT STEVE TREVOR DOWN!
OKAY.
AYYYIIIIII!
I'M ALWAYS FALLING FOR YOU. I MEAN, YOU'RE ALWAYS CATCHING ME!
LIKE, I MEAN, YOU'RE A GOOD SUPER HERO AND I LIKE HOW BRAVE AND HOW STRONG YOU ARE...
I MEAN, THANK YOU.
YOU'RE WELCOME!
WOW! GO, WONDER WOMAN!

I'LL GET YOU, SUPER HEROES!
WHOOM!

NOT IF I GET YOU FIRST.
HEY! STOP THAT, BIRD-BRAIN!
YOU'RE GONNA GET CRUSHED LIKE A BUG!
JUST CALM DOWN AND COME WITH US.

I NEVER SURRENDER!
THIS IS LOIS LANE REPORTING LIVE FROM THE SCENE OF GIGANTA'S ATTACK!
HD
KRANG!
HAWKGIRL IS HEROICALLY HOLDING BACK GIGANTA!
HD
GIGANTA IS ON THE MOVE!
HD
LOOKS LIKE SHE'S HEADING FOR CENTENNIAL PARK!
STAY AWAY, SUPERS!
CRASH!

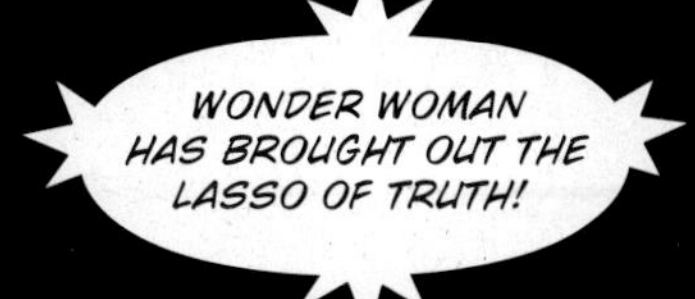
WONDER WOMAN HAS BROUGHT OUT THE LASSO OF TRUTH!
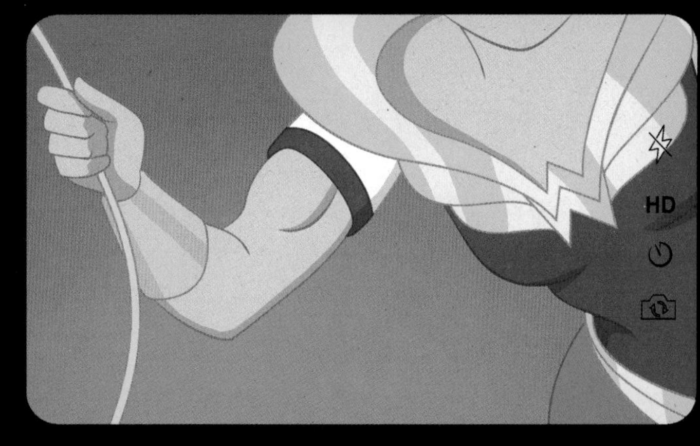
FANS WILL RECALL THAT WONDER WOMAN HOLDS THE ALL-TIME LASSOING RECORD.

SHE AIMS FOR GIGANTA...

...AND SHE THROWS!
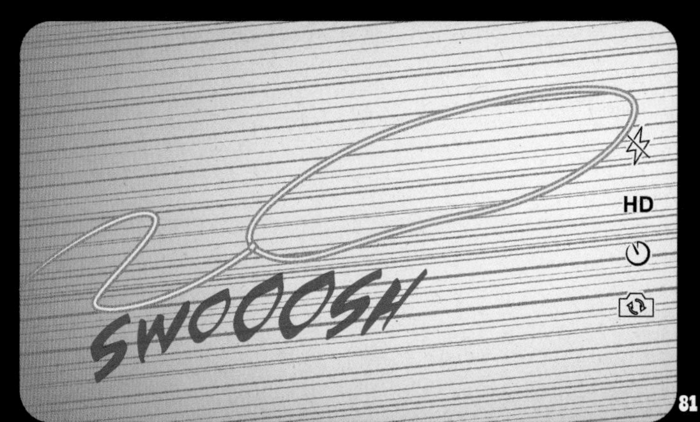
SWOOOSH

THUDDDDD
DOOOoOoOOM!

ARE WE SAFE?
ABSOLUTELY! NO ONE CAN ESCAPE MY LASSO. NOT EVEN ME!
I'VE GOT IT FROM HERE, GIRLS!
THANKS, COMMISSIONER!
OUR EXTRA CREDIT WORK HERE IS DONE!
WE'D BETTER GET BACK TO SUPER HERO HIGH SO WE CAN GET A GOOD NIGHT'S REST BEFORE FINALS IN THE MORNING.
COME ALONG, GIRLS.
ACTUALLY, I'M GOING TO STAY OUT A BIT LONGER. GIGANTA WORKED UP MY APPETITE FOR CRIME-FIGHTING.
MAYBE I'LL FIND ANOTHER VILLAIN!
YOU SHOULD NOT PURSUE VILLAINS AT THIS HOUR ALONE. THAT IS THE LONER, VIGILANTE WAY.
SUPER HERO HIGH RULE NUMBER 37, SECTION 2B STATES THAT ALL AFTER-HOUR VILLAIN NABBING MUST BE DONE IN A GROUP OF TWO OR MORE.
IT'S THE BUDDY SYSTEM.
I'M JUST HAVING FUN! I DON'T NEED A BUDDY TO HAVE FUN.
DON'T WAIT UP FOR ME!

THIS IS METROPOLIS. THERE HAS TO BE SOME CRIME TO STOP.
BANK ROBBERY? TRAFFIC VIOLATION? ANYTHING?
METROPOLIS BANK
YOU HEAR ABOUT ANY CRIME, PUPSTER?
HELP! SOMEBODY HELP ME!
STEVE? I'M COMING FOR YOU!
HELP! SOMEBODY HELP ME!
HELP! SOMEBODY HELP ME!
CORP
SUPPLY
STEVE! WHERE ARE YOU?
HELP! SOMEBODY HELP ME!

LEXCORP GARDEN SUPPL
WHAT IS THIS?
LEXCORP GARDEN SUPPLY
WHAT IS *THAT?!*
THE INESCAPABLE LASSO OF ***TRUTH!*** NIFTY!
TO BE CONTINUED.

chapter seven

KEEPING THE PEACE AND QUIET

MY MOTTO IS:
ALWAYS BE READY.
AND I'M READY FOR ***ANYTHING.***
I'M HERE TO HELP YOU. ¡ESTOY AQUÍ PARA AYUDARTE!
¡ESTOY AQUÍ PARA AYUDARTE!
BWOP!
WUB WUB WUB!
BWOP!

BWOP! WUB WUB WUB! BWOP!
HARLEY!
HA HA HA HA HA
HIYA, BATS! YOU'RE GONNA HAFTA SPEAK UP! I CAN'T HEAR YOU OVER THE MUSIC!
BWOP! WUB! WUB! WUB! WUB! BWOP!
I NEED YOU TO KEEP THE MUSIC DOWN SO I CAN STUDY FOR FINALS.
BUT IT'S DUBSTEP! YOU'RE SUPPOSED TO CRANK IT UP TO ELEVEN AND LET IT RATTLE YOUR INNARDS! PULL UP A WHOOPEE CUSHION AND ENJOY IT WITH ME?
NO THANKS, HARLEY. I NEED TO PREPARE FOR FINALS.
BUT YOU'RE THE MOST PREPARED GIRL IN SCHOOL!
WHATCHA NEED NOW IS A LITTLE R.N.R.N.R.N.R.-- REST 'N' RELAXATION 'N' ROCK'N'ROLL!
WHAT I NEED NOW IS SOME PEACE AND QUIET!

WUB!
WUB!
WUB!
WUB
I CAN'T STUDY HERE.
ZIPPPPPP
WOOOO!

POW! STUDYING ON!
YOU'LL BE MY MOST MASSIVE PLANT EVER!
READY OR NOT, HERE I COME!
FOUND YOU, BEAST BOY!
ERRRR!
THIS NOISE IS MAKING ME BATTY!
SOOOSSH!
KRINK!
ZZZRRR!
IF I'M GOING TO GET THE PEACE AND QUIET I NEED, NONE OF THE REGULAR STUDY SPOTS WILL DO. I HAVE TO GO EXTREME.

ZOOOOOOOOOM

BEEP!
BABS! I SAW THE BATPLANE LEAVING SCHOOL!

WHY AREN'T YOU STUDYING?
I'M TRYING TO, DAD!

IT WAS TOO LOUD THERE!

"BUT DON'T WORRY. I'M HEADED TO THE PERFECT STUDY SPOT!"

WELCOME, BATGIRL.

TO--

--THE--

--BATCAVE!
TOLD YOU I WAS READY FOR ANYTHING.

CAVE SWEET CAVE.
THUDDD!
GAH!
EVEN HERE?!
I WAS *PREPARED* FOR THIS. TO THE BETA BATCAVE!

MY BACKUP TO MY BATCAVE. I HAVE A FEW AROUND TOWN.
FINALLY, I CAN STUDY.
CLANK! CLANK! CLANK!
WHAT'S GOING ON UP THERE?
KLANG!
ELEPHANTS *PLAYING* FOOTBALL?
GARDEN SUPPL

MY LAST RESORT.
IT'S RISKY, BUT IT'S MY ONLY COMPLETELY SOUNDPROOF BATCAVE.
THE DOWNSIDE IS IT'S ONLY ACCESSIBLE THROUGH ONE HIDDEN PASSAGEWAY.
THE FACULTY LOUNGE WOULD USUALLY BE EMPTY AT THIS TIME OF NIGHT, BUT SINCE IT'S THE END OF THE SEMESTER, SOME HARD-NOSED TEACHER IS STILL THERE GRADING PAPERS.
FACULTY ONLY!
NO STUDENTS

A HARD-NOSED TEACHER WITH NO TOLERANCE FOR RULE-BREAKING WHO ALSO HAPPENS TO BE MY DAD.
HE WOULDN'T EXACTLY BE THRILLED WITH MY BUILDING A BATCAVE UNDERNEATH THE FACULTY LOUNGE.
RRRING!
COMMISSIONER GORDON HERE... SOLOMON GRUNDY DOWNTOWN?! I'LL BE RIGHT THERE!
SAVED BY THE CALL.
AT LAST, THE COMMON WATER COOLER!

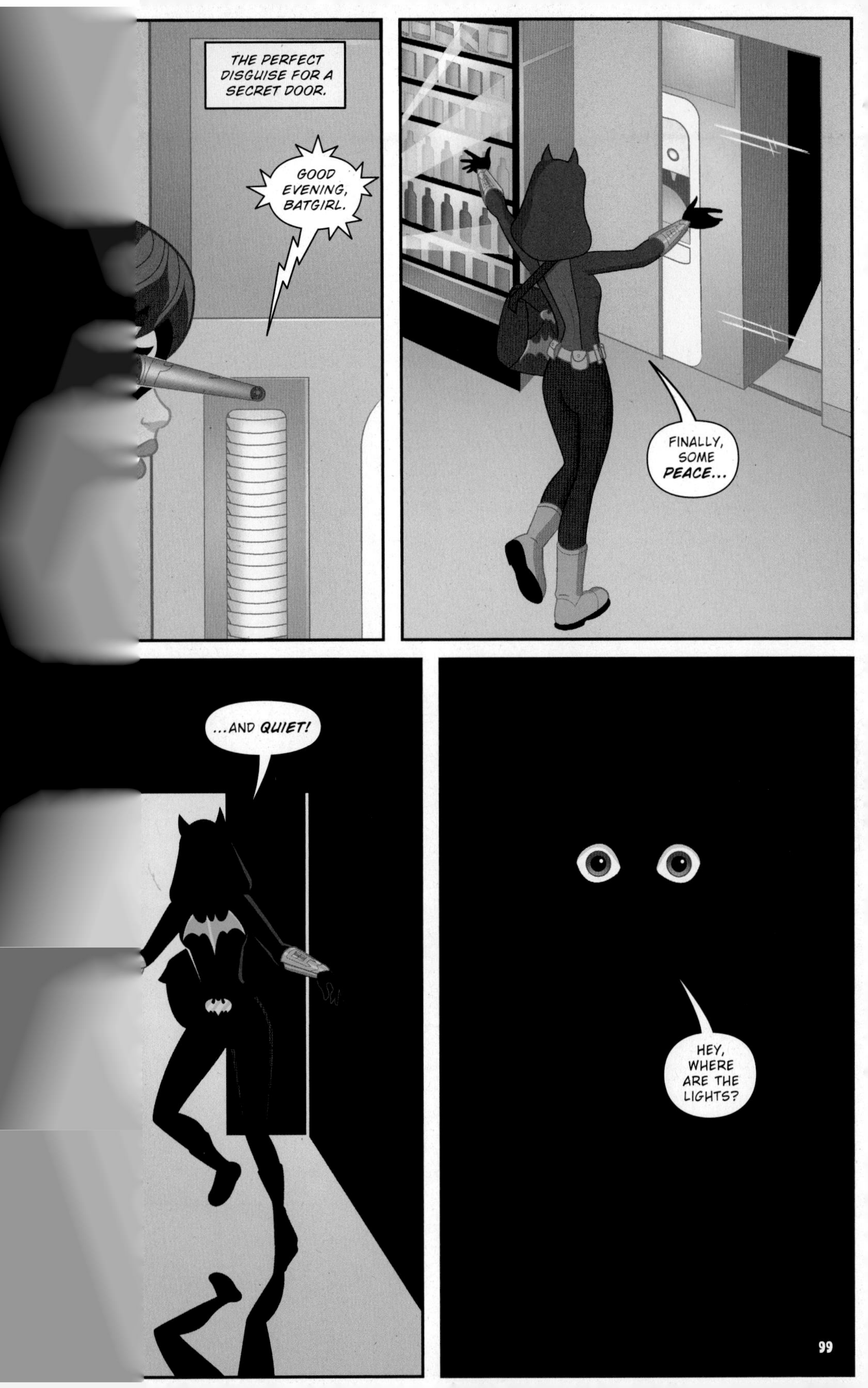
THE PERFECT DISGUISE FOR A SECRET DOOR.
GOOD EVENING, BATGIRL.
FINALLY, SOME PEACE...
...AND QUIET!
HEY, WHERE ARE THE LIGHTS?

LUCKILY, I BROUGHT A FLASHLIGHT. I DON'T NEED IT, THOUGH--INFRARED NIGHT GOGGLES!
WHAT? WHO ARE YOU? WHAT'S GOING ON?
CRASH!
KRRACK!
UGH!
LET GO OF ME! HELP!
BANG!
NO ONE CAN HEAR YOU. THAT'S YOUR OWN SOUNDPROOFING TECH! HEY, MAYBE YOU CAN SHOW ME HOW TO SOUNDPROOF MY LAIR?
SUPERGIRL
WONDER WOMAN
BUMBLEBEE
KATANA
BATGIRL
IVY
TO BE CONTINUED.

chapter eight

BLONDES HAVE MORE FUN

BWOP!
BWOP!
THERE I WAS, MINDING MY OWN BEESWAX.
HARLEY!
BUT THIS GIRLY WANTED TO PUT THE KIBOSH ON MY FUN.
OUR BRAIN BUCKETS ARE FILLED TO OVERFLOWIN' WITH FACTS, FIGURES, AND CITIZEN-SAVIN' SCENARIOS.

MY FELLOW SUPER HERO HIGH-ERS ARE ALREADY SMARTER THAN YOUR AVERAGE CHIMPANZEE.
NOW ISN'T THE TIME FOR MORE BOOK LEARNIN'.
NOW IS THE TIME TO RELAX AND HAVE A LITTLE FUN!
WHICH IS WHY I'M SELFLESSLY GIVIN' BACK TO THE STUDENT BODY BY SHARING MY EXPERTISE.

Let's PaRty HaRLey!!!
WHere? MY RooM
WheN? AFter SCHool
PAR-
-TAY!

IT'S GONNA BE A BLAST!
WHADDYA SAY, FROST? CAN I COUNT YOUR R.S.V.P. AS A Y.E.S.?
YEAH, SOUNDS COOL!
A PARTY?
EEP!
BUT, HARLEY, IS NOT THE WEEKDAY PARTY AGAINST THE RULES AND THE REGULATIONS OF PRINCIPAL WALLER?
IF SHE'S NOT PRIVY TO MY PARTY, THEN THERE'S NO RISK OF RUFFLIN' HER RULE-ENFORCIN' FEATHERS.

FINALS PARTY?
SOUNDS PURR-FECT!
YEAH!
WELL, GREEN LANTERN, ARE YOU GOING TO ASK ME TO HARLEY'S PARTY OR WHAT?
OH YEAH!
HEY, STAR SAPPHIRE, WANNA GO TO HARLEY'S PARTY WITH ME?
HAL
I'LL THINK ABOUT IT.
I'M RECEIVING A MESSAGE. I SEE BALLOONS, DANCING-- A PARTY! RED AND BLACK. WHAT COULD IT MEAN?
HARLEY PARTY!
DON'T INTERRUPT ME WHEN I'M PSYCHIC-ING!

HA
HA
HA
HA
HA
HA
HA
AT THE POP OF THIS BALLOON, WE'LL OFFICIALLY GET THIS PARTY START--
HOLD THE PHONE! WHERE'S IVY?
HA
WHERE'RE BUMBLEBEE AND KATANA?
AND SUPERGIRL, BATGIRL, AND WONDY?
WHERE MY GIRLS AT?!

BAM!
NO WAY AM I HAVING A PARTY WITHOUT MY MAIN GAL-PALS!
BATGIRL, SORRY I TURNED UP THE MUSIC AGAIN, BUT YOU DON'T HAVE TO HIDE OUT.
BATS?
KATANA?
BUMBLEBEE!

THERE'S SOMETHING FUNNY HAPPENING IN METROPOLIS AND NOBODY DOES FUNNY WITHOUT HARLEY QUINN!
RINNG!
SHUT OFF THAT ALARM! I'M TRYING TO THINK.
RINNG!
TRYIN' TO GET AWAY FROM ME?
YOU'RE GONNA GET POPPED, PUDDIN'!

RINNG! RINNG!
METROPOLIS BANK
SOLOMON GRUNDY?
HOLD IT RIGHT THERE, SLOWPOKE!
$
$

UGH!
POWF!
$

TELL ME WHAT YOU DID WITH MY FRIENDS, OR I GOT ANOTHER GLITTER BOMB WITH YOUR NAME ON IT!
SOLOMON GRUNDY DON'T KNOW ABOUT ANY FRIENDS! SOLOMON GRUNDY JUST WANT TO ROB BANK!
$
IVY'S BEEN HERE!
I'M COMING FOR YOU, GIRLIES!

HUFF! HUFF!
LEXCORP GARDEN SUPPLY
LEXCORP GARDEN SUPPLY? IVY FELL FOR THAT?!
HYPOTHETICALLY SPEAKIN', IF I WERE TO GO INTO VILLAINY, I'D TRY A LITTLE HARDER WITH MY SCHEMES!
GRRRR!
OPEN UP AND GIVE ME BACK MY *FRIENDS!*
OR YOU'LL FACE THE WRATH OF HARLEY QUINN!
MEGA SALE!!! 50%
WHAM!

WHO'S THAT?
OH NO! HARLEY!
HARLEY QUINN? HOW DID SHE FIND US?
OH, HARLEY IS SMART!
AND SHE'S REALLY STRONG!
SO YOU'D BETTER JUST LET US GO BEFORE SHE COMES DOWN HERE AND MAKES YOU WILT!
HA HA! AND I THOUGHT HARLEY WAS SUPPOSED TO BE THE FUNNY ONE!
PERHAPS I UNDERESTIMATED THE COMPLEXITY OF TEENAGE GIRLS.
SHE DIDN'T MAKE MY FIRST CUT, BUT I DON'T MIND ADDING HARLEY TO THE GUEST LIST!

LET ME--
K-CHUNK
--INNNNNNNN!

HOW'D YOU FIND US?
SORRY TO *DROP IN* ON YOU!
WHEN YOU DIDN'T SHOW UP FOR MY BASH, I WENT LOOKING...
C'MON. LET'S FIGURE OUT HOW TO GET OUT OF HERE!
...BUT I SEE YOU'VE BEEN HAVING SOME SORTA KRYPTONITE-POWERED PRISON PARTY WITHOUT ME!
TO BE CONCLUDED.

chapter nine

FINALS COUNTDOWN

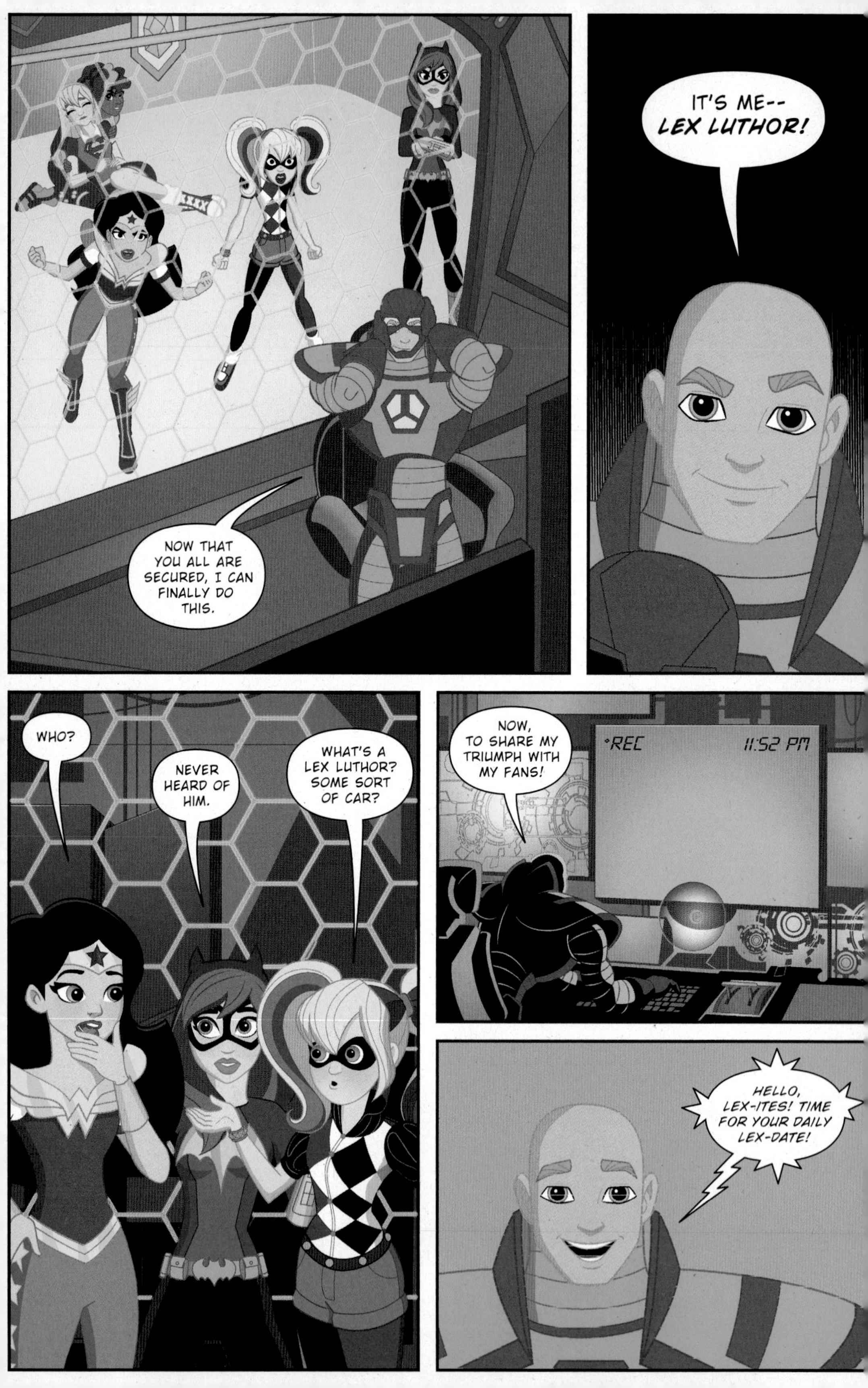
NOW THAT YOU ALL ARE SECURED, I CAN FINALLY DO THIS.
IT'S ME-- LEX LUTHOR!
WHO?
NEVER HEARD OF HIM.
WHAT'S A LEX LUTHOR? SOME SORT OF CAR?
NOW, TO SHARE MY TRIUMPH WITH MY FANS!
•REC
11:52 PM
HELLO, LEX-ITES! TIME FOR YOUR DAILY LEX-DATE!

SHOUT OUT TO MY LITTLE SISTER, WHO WAS MY INSPIRATION FOR MY FIRST BIG MISSION!
WITH THIS SUIT SHE BUILT, I TOOK DOWN THE TOP SUPERS IN METROPOLIS!
TO GET OUT OF HERE, WE NEED OUTSIDE HELP.
BUT THERE'S SOMETHING SCRAMBLING OUR COMM BRACELETS--
NOT THAT KIND OF OUTSIDE. I MEANT ***IVY'S*** KIND OF ***OUTSIDE.***
BUT, THERE ARE NO PLANTS IN HERE. MY POWERS AREN'T STRONG ENOUGH TO REACH THE PLANTS OUTSIDE.
I'M ON IT, IVY. I THINK I CAN BUILD A POWER AMPLIFIER.
HOURS LATER...
...WHEN SUPER HERO HIGH REJECTED HER APPLICATION, SHE TOOK IT REALLY HARD.
BUT NOW I HAVE THEIR TOP STUDENTS! WITH THESE GIRLS OFF THE ROSTER, THERE'LL BE PLENTY OF ROOM FOR ONE LUTHOR!
MY SIS IS GOING TO BE SO STOKED WHEN SHE HEARS WHAT I DID!

SUPER HERO HIGH WILL BE SO DESPERATE FOR NEW STUDENTS THAT THEY WON'T EVEN CARE THAT SHE FAILED THE PSYCH TEST!
YOWZA. EVEN I PASSED THE PSYCH TEST.
THIS PLACE IS SO SECURE. HOW WILL I GET A BIG PLANT INSIDE?
WE DON'T NEED BIG. WE NEED STEALTH! I HAVE AN IDEA...

...SO THAT'S HOW I GOT HERE! I'M RECORDING THIS SO YOU'LL UNDERSTAND.
WHEN MY SISTER'S THE GREATEST SUPER IN THE WORLD, YOU'LL THANK ME.
I'M NOT THE BAD GUY HERE. THE PEOPLE WHO REJECTED HER IN THE FIRST PLACE ARE THE BAD GUYS!
YANK!
FZZZZT!
I'M THE GOOD GUY--THE ONE SETTING THINGS RIGHT!
HUH?
8:52 AM

BUMBLEBEE! YOUR BATTERY!
AND I'LL TAKE THIS BACK!
MAYBE YOUR SUIT WAS POWERFUL ENOUGH TO DEFEAT US ONE-ON-ONE.
BUT WE'RE STRONGER WHEN WE WORK TOGETHER!
YOU CAN'T DEFEAT THIS TEAM!

NO BULLY WILL KEEP ME FROM MY FINALS!
LET'S GET THIS PARTY STARTED!
POP!
HEY!

ALERT METROPOLIS S.C.U. THAT WE NEED A VILLAIN PICKUP!
AS YOU WISH, BATGIRL.
NO! MY SISTER WILL GET YOU FOR THIS!
APPOINTMENT REMINDER. FINALS COMMENCING IN ONE MINUTE.
C'MON, GIRLS!
WOOOOOOOOSH!
SORRY, STUDENTS. IT'S 9:01. NO LATE ENTRIES ALLOWED.

BUT PRINCIPAL WALLER! HEAR US OUT!
I WAS ON MY WAY BACK FROM THE KENT'S AND HE SHOT ME WITH KRYPTONITE!
I WAS ALONE AND HE TOOK MY LASSO!
AFTER I FIXED THE SMOOTHIE MACHINE, I COULD SMELL ALL THESE HONEY TREATS!
I PUT YOUR TROPHY BACK AND THERE HE WAS!
I NEEDED THE FERTILIZER FOR MY NEW SUPER-PLANT PROJECT.
I JUST WANTED TO PARTY!
THE RULES CLEARLY STATE THAT NO *LATE* DEMONSTRATIONS ARE PERMITTED.
BATGIRL! I WAS SEARCHING FOR LEADS AND I STUMBLED ON THIS VIDEO THAT SOMEONE WAS STREAMING. LOOK FAMILIAR?
LOIS?

BUT THE RULES DON'T SAY ANYTHING ABOUT HAVING TO DO IT HERE.
WE WEREN'T LATE--WE JUST WEREN'T HERE! LOOK AT THE VIDEO!
THIS SHOWS THAT OUR POWERS HAVE IMPROVED SINCE WE STARTED AT SUPER HERO HIGH.
YEAH! WHEN WE STARTED SCHOOL HERE, WE WERE ALONE.
BUT NOW WE'RE A *TEAM.*
AND TOGETHER OUR POWERS ARE GREATER THAN EVER BEFORE!
I AGREE.
YAY!

BUT YOU ALL JUST ADMITTED TO BREAKING THE RULES YESTERDAY, SO THAT'S THREE WEEKS DETENTION.
NO FAIR!
REALLY?!
AGAIN?
NO GRUMBLIN' IN DETENTION!
CONGRATULATIONS ON PASSING YOUR FINALS! WELCOME TO YOUR SECOND SEMESTER!
HOPE YOU'RE READY, BECAUSE THINGS ARE ABOUT TO GET REALLY SUPER...
THE END.

about the

AUTHOR

Shea Fontana is a writer for film, television, and graphic novels. Her credits include *DC Super Hero Girls* animated shorts, television specials, and movies, *Dorothy and the Wonders of Oz, Doc McStuffins, The 7D, Whisker Haven Tales with the Palace Pets, Disney on Ice,* and the feature film *Crowning Jules.* She lives in sunny Los Angeles where she enjoys playing roller derby, hiking, hanging out with her dog, Moxie, and changing her hair color. ★

about the

COLORIST

Monica Kubina has colored countless comics, including super hero series, manga titles, kids comics, and science fiction stories. She's colored *Phineas and Ferb, SpongeBob, THE 99,* and *Star Wars.* Monica's favorite activities are bike riding and going to museums with her husband and two young sons. ★

about the

Yancey Labat got his start at Marvel Comics before moving on to illustrate children's books from *Hello Kitty* to *Peanuts* for Scholastic, as well as books for Chronicle Books, ABC Mouse, and others. His book *How Many Jellybeans?* with writer Andrea Menotti won the 2013 Cook Prize for best STEM (Science, Technology, Education, Math) picture book from Bank Street College of Education. He has two super hero girls of his own and lives in Cupertino, California. ★

about the

Janice Chiang has lettered *Archie, Barbie, Punisher* and many more. She was the first woman to win the Comic Buyer's Guide Fan Awards for Best Letterer (2011). She likes weight training, hiking, baking, gardening, and traveling. ★